Quicker Than a Princess

By Enid Richemont

Licensed exclusively to Top That Publishing Ltd
Tide Mill Way, Woodbridge, Suffolk, IP12 1AP, UK
www.topthatpublishing.com
Copyright © 2014 Tide Mill Media
All rights reserved
2 4 6 8 9 7 5 3 1

Illustrated by Inna Chernyak
Written by Enid Richemont

ISBN 978-1-78445-189-9

A catalogue record for this book is available from the British Library
Manufactured in China

'For David Richemont,
Stargazer and Scholar'

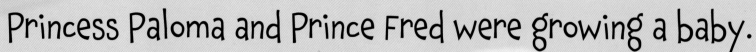

Princess Paloma and Prince Fred were growing a baby.

Love plus love makes babies.

But people babies take a long time to grow.

In a meadow full of daisies,
Emma Ewe was growing TWO babies.

A baa plus a baa makes two sheep babies.

In twenty weeks, there were two little lambs.
'I'm quicker than a princess,' said Emma Ewe.

In a tree, Susie Squirrel
was growing THREE babies.

A snuffle plus a cuddle makes
three squirrel babies.

In just six weeks, there were three little pups.
'I'm quicker than a princess,' said Susie Squirrel.

In a barn, Chloe Cat was growing FOUR babies.

A miaow plus a purr
makes pussycat babies.

In just eight weeks, there were kittens in the barn.
'I'm quicker than a princess,' said Chloe Cat.

In a bush, Betty Blackbird was growing FIVE babies.

A song plus a song makes five blackbird babies.

In just two weeks, five little chicks hatched.
'I'm quicker than a princess,' sang Betty Blackbird.

Prince Fred and Princess Paloma had their baby.
It took them nine whole months to grow Baby Joe.
They wrapped him in a blanket and sat him in the sun.
Warm milk and cuddles make a happy, happy baby.

Emma Ewe came to visit,
with her two little lambs.
'That's only ONE baby,' sniffed
Emma. 'But it's a nice baby.'

Susie Squirrel looked down,
with her three little pups.
'That's just ONE baby,' said Susie
Squirrel. 'But it's a pretty baby.'

Chloe Cat came over with her four little kittens.
'Only ONE baby?' said Chloe Cat. 'But it is a sweet baby.'

Betty Blackbird sang Joe a lullaby.
'You're a pretty baby,' she thought.
'Maybe one day you'll fly.'

Down at the zoo, Ellie Elephant
was growing a baby.
Two trumpets and two trunks
make an elephant baby.
It's been six hundred days,
and it's not ready yet!

'I was quicker than an elephant!' smiled Princess Paloma.